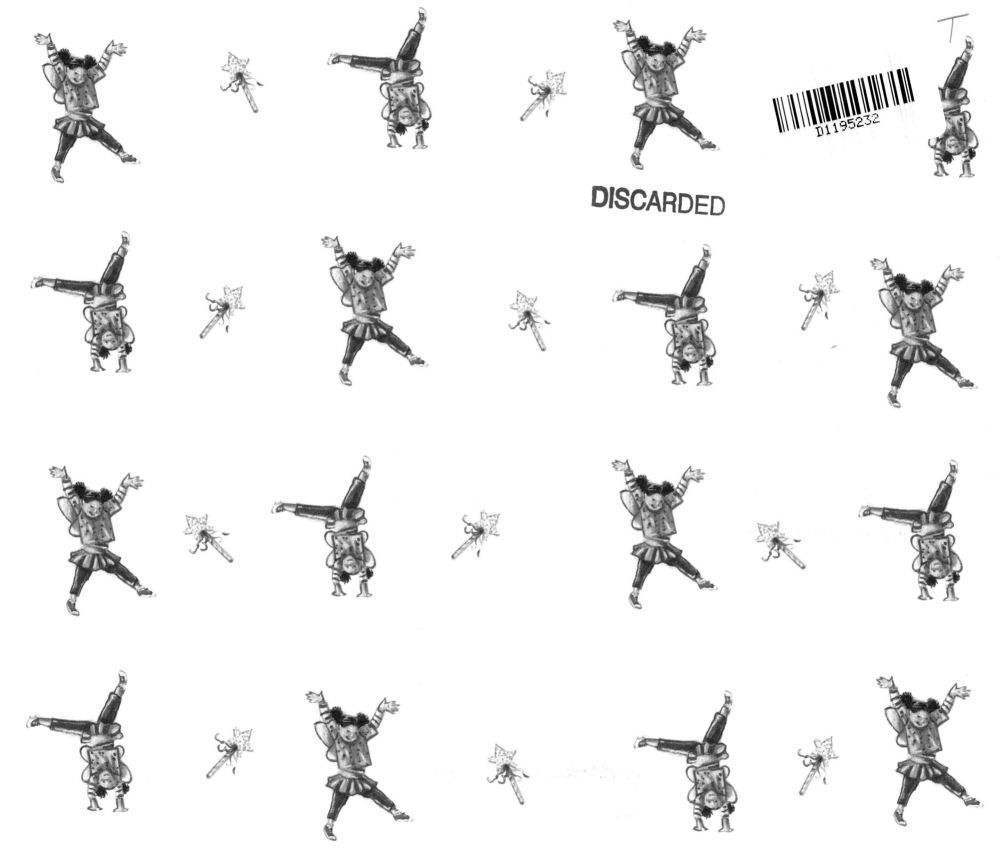

DISCARDED

Amazingly Wonderful Things

Written by Marla J. Hohmeier

Illustrated by Penny Weber

For my mom Jean, my daughter Akeila, and Morgan—our magical Padorgan. I love you all so much. ✳ *Marla*

For Doug, Keith and Erica. ✳ *Penny*

Hohmeier, Marla J.

    Amazingly Wonderful Things / written by Marla J. Hohmeier; illustrated by Penny Weber
—1st ed. —McHenry, IL: Raven Tree Press, 2011.

    p. ; cm.

    SUMMARY: When a child's imagination is set free every child is capable of amazingly wonderful things.

    English Edition
    ISBN 978-1-936299-10-2 hardcover

    Audience: pre-K to 3rd grade
    Title available in English-only

        1. Imagination and Play—Juvenile fiction. 2. Fantasy—Juvenile fiction.
        I. Illust. Weber, Penny. II. Title.

        Library of Congress Control Number: 2010936671

        Printed in Taiwan
        10 9 8 7 6 5 4 3 2 1
        First Edition

Free activities for this book are available at www.raventreepress.com

PRINTED WITH SOY INK

Raven Tree Press
A Division of Delta Systems Co., Inc.
www.raventreepress.com

Amazingly
Wonderful Things

Written by Marla J. Hohmeier
Illustrated by Penny Weber

I can do amazingly wonderful things!

I can **ride** a shining star.

Star riding is like sitting at the top of a Ferris wheel made of diamonds.

I can **BOUNCE** across the ocean.

Ocean bouncing is like hopping
over a river of root beer floats.

I can *CLIMB* up a rainbow.

Rainbow climbing is like hiking up a mountain in a new pair of jelly-bean shoes.

I can **_RACE_** a supernova.

Supernova racing is like sprinting along a beach of rainbow sprinkles.

I can FLY with the wind.

Wind flying is like soaring through
silky feathers on a rose-petal kite.

12

I can *tiptoe* up a waterfall.

Waterfall tiptoeing is like hiding in a whipped-cream fountain.

14

I can *dance* in the stardust.

Stardust dancing is like twirling
in a gown made of fireflies.

16

I can **FLOAT** on a cloud.

Cloud floating is like swimming across
a sea of pink and blue cotton candy.

19

I can **cartwheel** down a sunbeam.

20

Sunbeam cartwheeling
is like somersaulting
down a
caramel-covered banana.

I can **PAINT** all of the raindrops.

Raindrop painting is like coloring all of the bubbles in a bubble bath.

22

I can **JUMP** on the moon.

Moon jumping is like leaping into a giant bowl filled with marshmallows.

24

I can **skate** on hot lava.

Lava skating is like sliding down a hot fudge sundae.

27

I can **splash** through the Milky Way.

28

Milky Way splashing is like puddle stomping in a pond of chocolate and vanilla milkshakes.

29

I can **run circles** around the sun.

Sun running is like chasing a fire-breathing dragon across the sky.

I can do amazingly wonderful things,
and *so* can you.